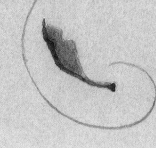

For Joan, my writing buddy
~CF

For Alex Abbey
~VC

LITTLE TIGER PRESS
An imprint of Magi Publications
1 The Coda Centre, 189 Munster Road
London SW6 6AW
www.littletigerpress.com

First published in Great Britain 2003

Printed in Italy by Grafiche AZ

10 9 8 7 6 5 4 3 2 1

Goose on the Loose

Claire Freedman

Vanessa Cabban

Little Tiger Press

London

The sun was up and shining.
Red and gold autumn leaves
tumbled from the trees.
"Wakey wakey, little Gooseberry!" called
Mama Goose. "It's lovely weather for
you to practise your flying again."
"Yippee!" Gooseberry replied,
leaping out of bed.

So, after breakfast, Gooseberry flip-flapped through
the fallen leaves, all the way down to the lake.
His friend Beaver was at work in the water, busily
swimming to and fro.
"Hey, Beaver," called Gooseberry. "Would you like
to watch me practise my take-off and landing?"

Gooseberry ran and ran,
as fast as he could, along the bank.
"Clear the runway! Goose on the loose!"
he shouted. "Vroom!"
He soared right over Beaver's head and
landed again with a bump!

"See that?" cried Gooseberry. "I'm getting better and better all the time!"
"Great landing!" agreed Beaver. "But I can't stop, Gooseberry. I must finish building my dam before winter comes." And with a quick wave, Beaver disappeared beneath the ripples.

Gooseberry zig-zagged through the air,
backwards and forwards across the lake. Orange
and yellow leaves tumbled from the trees.
"I bet I could dance in the breeze like the leaves,"
said Gooseberry. He decided to try.

"Up, up and away I go!" Gooseberry cried.
"Whoooosh!"
  It wasn't so easy. But someone was clapping!

"Great moves," called Gooseberry's friend, Red Squirrel.

"Watch me again!" said Gooseberry. "I can glide on the wind now!"

"Sorry, little Gooseberry, I've far too much work to do!" Red Squirrel replied. "I'm busy storing away food, before winter arrives." And Red Squirrel scampered away to bury his acorns.

As Gooseberry practised his swoops
and dives he spotted his friend Mouse.
"Look at my loop the loops, Mouse!"
he called. "I can do them at last!"

"That's clever!" said Mouse. "I've no
time to stop though. I'm in a hurry
to find some warm thistledown
for my nest. Don't you know . . ."
"Yes, I heard!" sighed Gooseberry.
"Winter's coming!"

"If you're really clever you'll start getting ready for winter too," Mouse called as she scurried off.

"Maybe Mouse is right," thought Gooseberry. "But I don't know where to begin."

Gooseberry started searching for berries and seeds, but it was hard work. "Phew! I'd rather practise flying!" he decided.

Fluffy white clouds scudded across the sky.
"I wonder how high I can fly?" thought
Gooseberry. Up, up, up the little goose
soared, and down, down, down he spiralled.
"Wheeee!" cried Gooseberry. "I couldn't do
that before!"
"That looked scary!" called Hare from the
muddy bank.

"Did you see how high I went?" Gooseberry laughed. "I can show you again, if you like!"
"Well, I'm hard at work tidying my burrow," Hare replied. "I must get it spick and span and cosy before snowy winter comes!"
And Hare hopped down his hole in a hurry.

Suddenly a little chilly breeze ruffled Gooseberry's feathers. He began to feel a teeny bit worried. Winter *was* coming! Everyone was preparing for it – except him. Perhaps he had better hurry up and do something – before it was too late! Gooseberry decided to fly back home at once.

"Whatever is the matter, Gooseberry?" Mama asked.
"Winter's coming!" Gooseberry cried. "And I'm
not ready!"
Mama Goose laughed. "Silly Gooseberry!" she said.
"Don't you remember me telling you? Geese don't
stay here for winter. Brrr no!"

"We'll be flying south, to where it's lovely and warm!" Papa Goose added. "It's a long journey, and that's why you needed to practise your flying. You *have* been getting ready for winter all along!"

"So I have!" said Gooseberry happily. "I bet I could fly for miles and miles. Just watch!" And little Gooseberry dipped and dived and danced in the fading blue sky. Just like the red and gold leaves that tumbled from the trees.